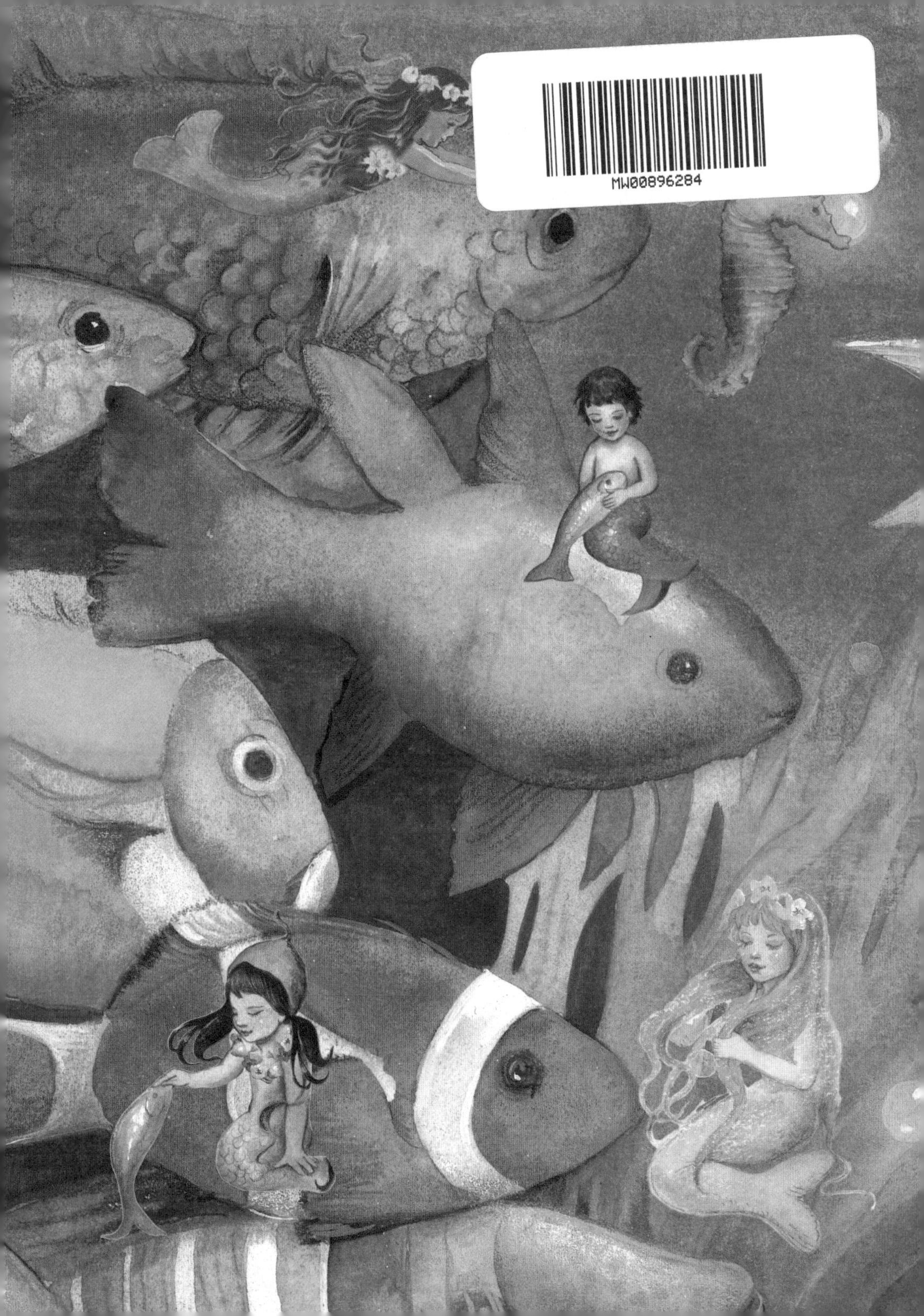

First North American edition published
in 2013 by Boxer Books Limited.
www.boxerbooks.com
Boxer® is a registered trademark of Boxer Books Limited

ISBN 978-1-907967-59-7

1 3 5 7 9 10 8 6 4 2

Printed in China

All of our papers are sourced from managed
forests and renewable resources.

# SECRET
# *Diaries*
# MERMAIDS

ILLUSTRATED BY
# BEVERLIE MANSON

BOXER BOOKS

# MERMAIDS' FAVORITE THINGS

Welcome to my secret diary.

This is where I keep all my private thoughts and favorite memories. Every mermaid should have a special place to keep things that are important to her. Shhh, keep it secret. And don't let it get wet!

Some of my favorite mermaid things:

Riding a dolphin

Watching the Northern Lights

Playing tag in the shallows

The full moon

Ice sculptures

What are your favorite things?

# MY FAVORITE THINGS

MY NAME

MY AGE

MY FAVORITE COLOR

A PHOTO OF ME

# MERMAIDS' NEW YEAR'S RESOLUTIONS

Dear Diary, Today is January 1st and we made resolutions.

I will take good care of the baby seals.

I will help look after the merbabies.

I will practice my diving. What are your New year's Resolutions?

# MY NEW YEAR'S RESOLUTIONS

# JANUARY

Today, Beatrice and I swam
with the giant fishes. It was
wonderful.

# JANUARY

Do you like swimming? What are your
favorite things to do in the water?

# JANUARY

Dear Diary,

Selena and I took the merbabies swimming this afternoon. It's fun watching them learn how to paddle. We had to make sure that no one was left behind. Nina got tired and had to hitch a ride from a seal!

# JANUARY

Which of your New year's
Resolutions have you kept?

# FEBRUARY

Dear Diary,

Tomorrow is the Mermaid Ball. We have one every Valentine's Day. There is always a competition to see who can sing the best duet. I think Kallyn and Ethan will win again.

# FEBRUARY

I would like to wear something special to the Ball. Maybe I'll make a scarf of silver seaweed and wear it around my shoulders.

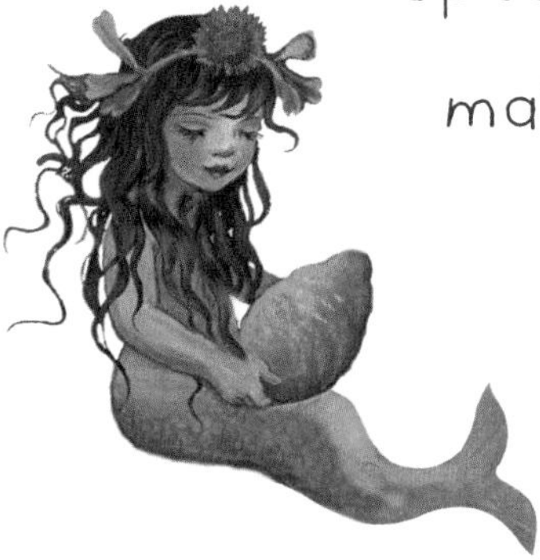

I still have to find a partner! I'm going to braid my hair with sea grass and wear a coral headdress. Are you doing anything special on Valentine's Day?

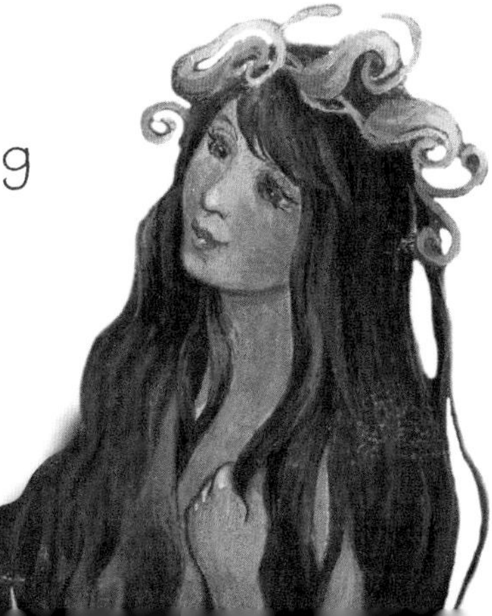

# ♥ FEBRUARY ♥

## MY SECRET ADMIRERS

Shhh. Don't tell. I got a Valentine's card, but I don't know who it's from!

Will you be sending any Valentines? Who will you send them to?

16

# VALENTINE

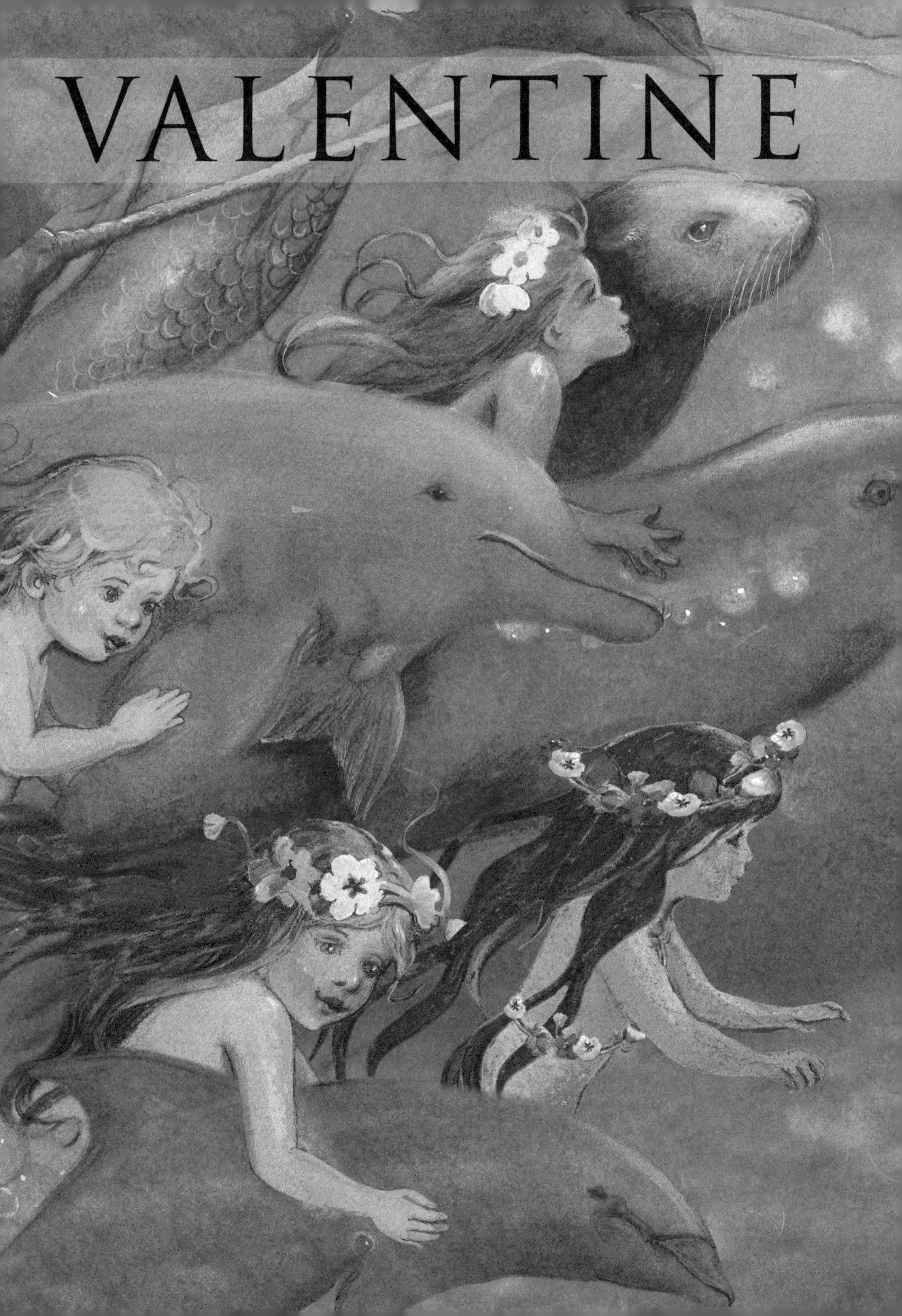

# FEBRUARY

Dear Diary,
It's freezing in the water at the
moment, but we mermaids have
secret ways to keep warm.
We cuddle up with the polar bears.
They have such thick, warm fur.

# FEBRUARY

How do you keep warm in winter?
Hot water bottles, warm baths, hot
chocolate? Write a few of the best
ways here:

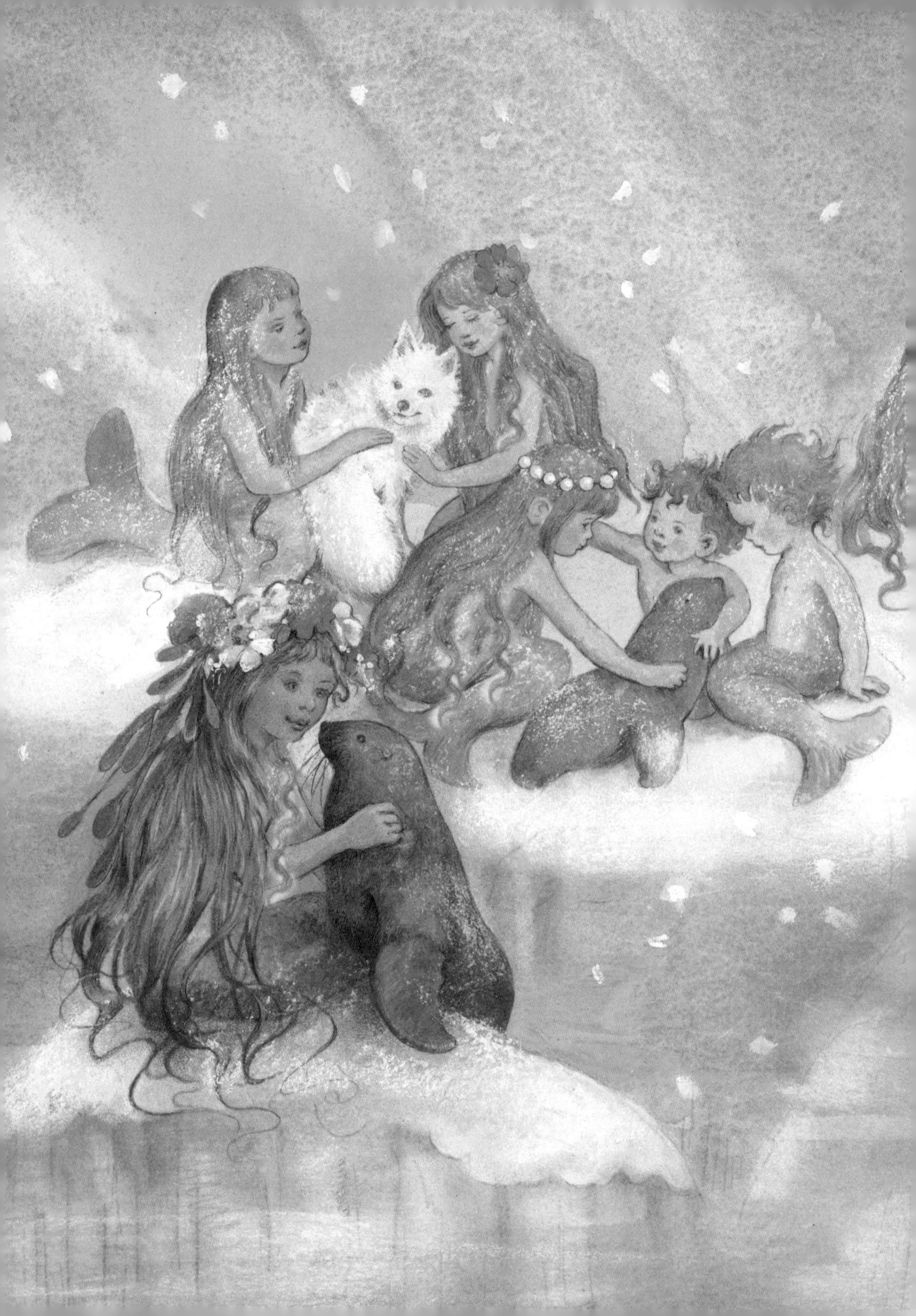

# FEBRUARY

Guess what? This evening there is going to be a full moon! All the merpeople get together and sing to welcome it. The foxes and seals join the party. They love a good sing-along!
What are your favorite songs?

# SPRING

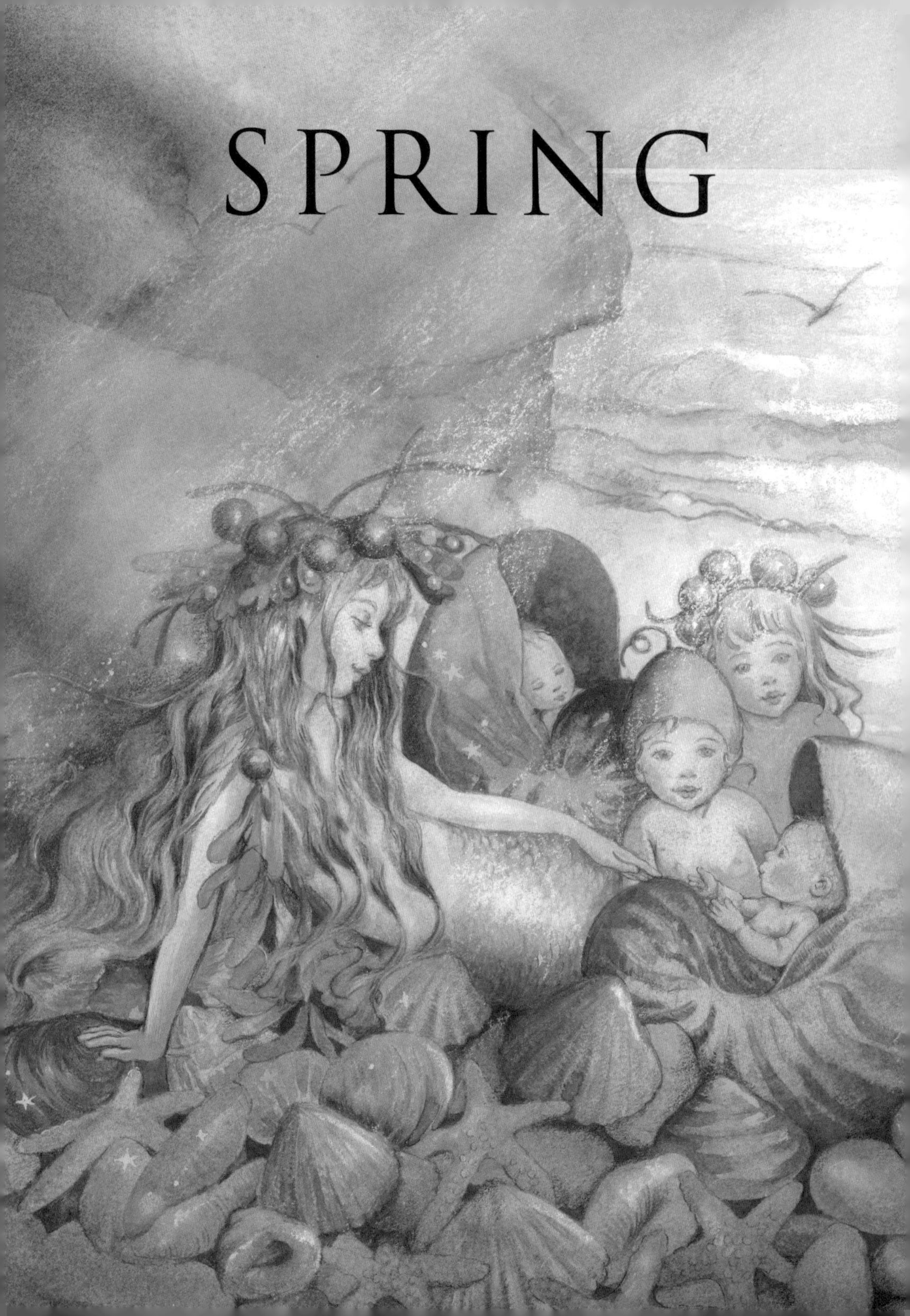

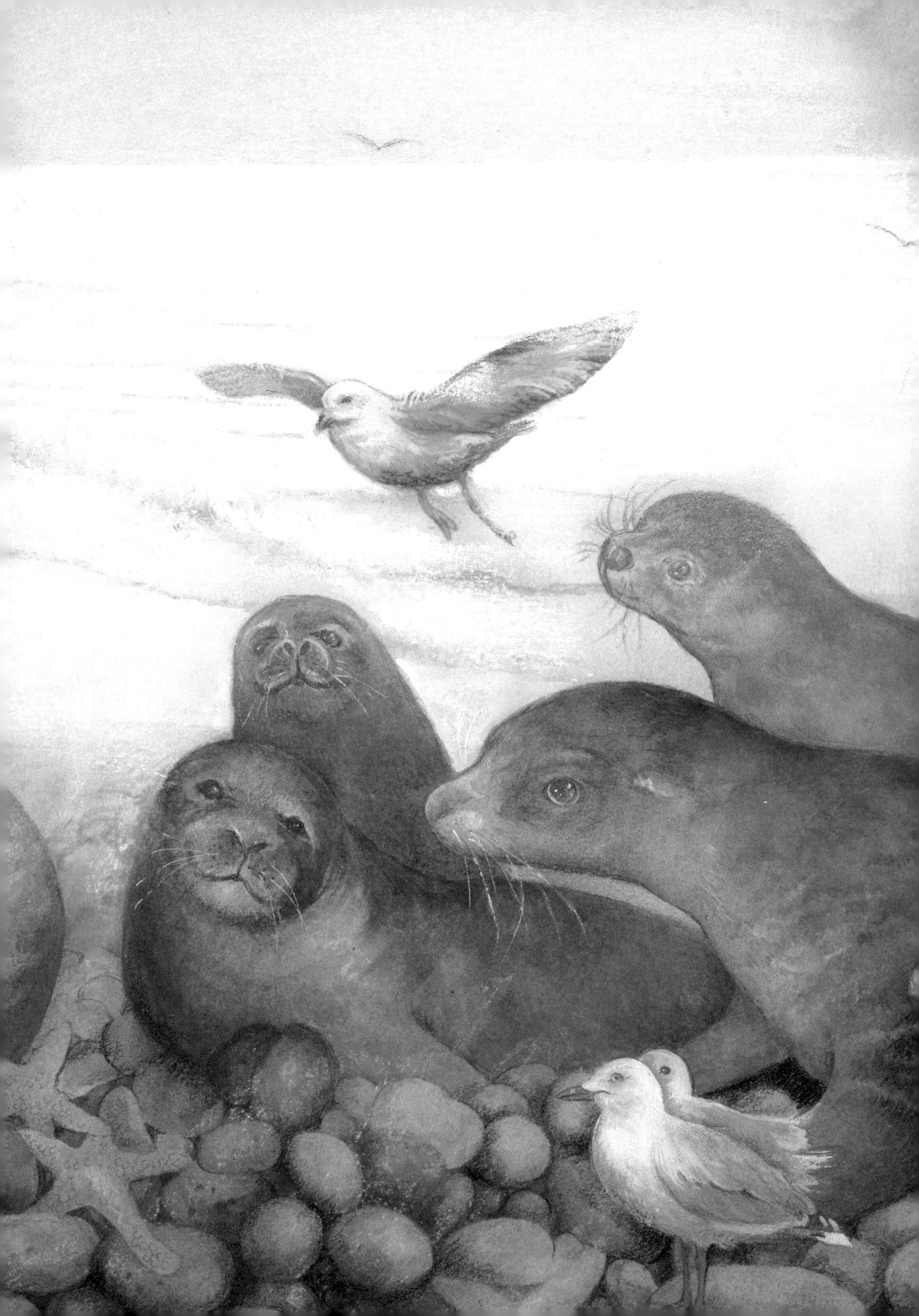

# MARCH

Dear Diary,

It's springtime – at last! Time to
clean the coral reefs, collect the silver
seaweed, and make pretty jewelry from
different-colored sea shells.

# MARCH

Do you have a sea shell collection? How do you like to display it? Draw a picture of your favorite shells:

# MARCH

Dear Diary,
This morning we explored
a shipwreck. It was
thrilling. Coral found an
old treasure chest full
of precious stones.

Coral is so kind.
She shared her
treasure with
everyone.

# MARCH

What can you share with
your friends?

# MARCH

Did you know when you see bubbles
on the surface of the sea, there is a
merbaby somewhere giggling? Shhh.
Keep it a secret.

Do you have any secrets? you can share
one here:

# MARCH

Will you be coloring Easter eggs? Draw us a picture of your most beautiful Easter egg:

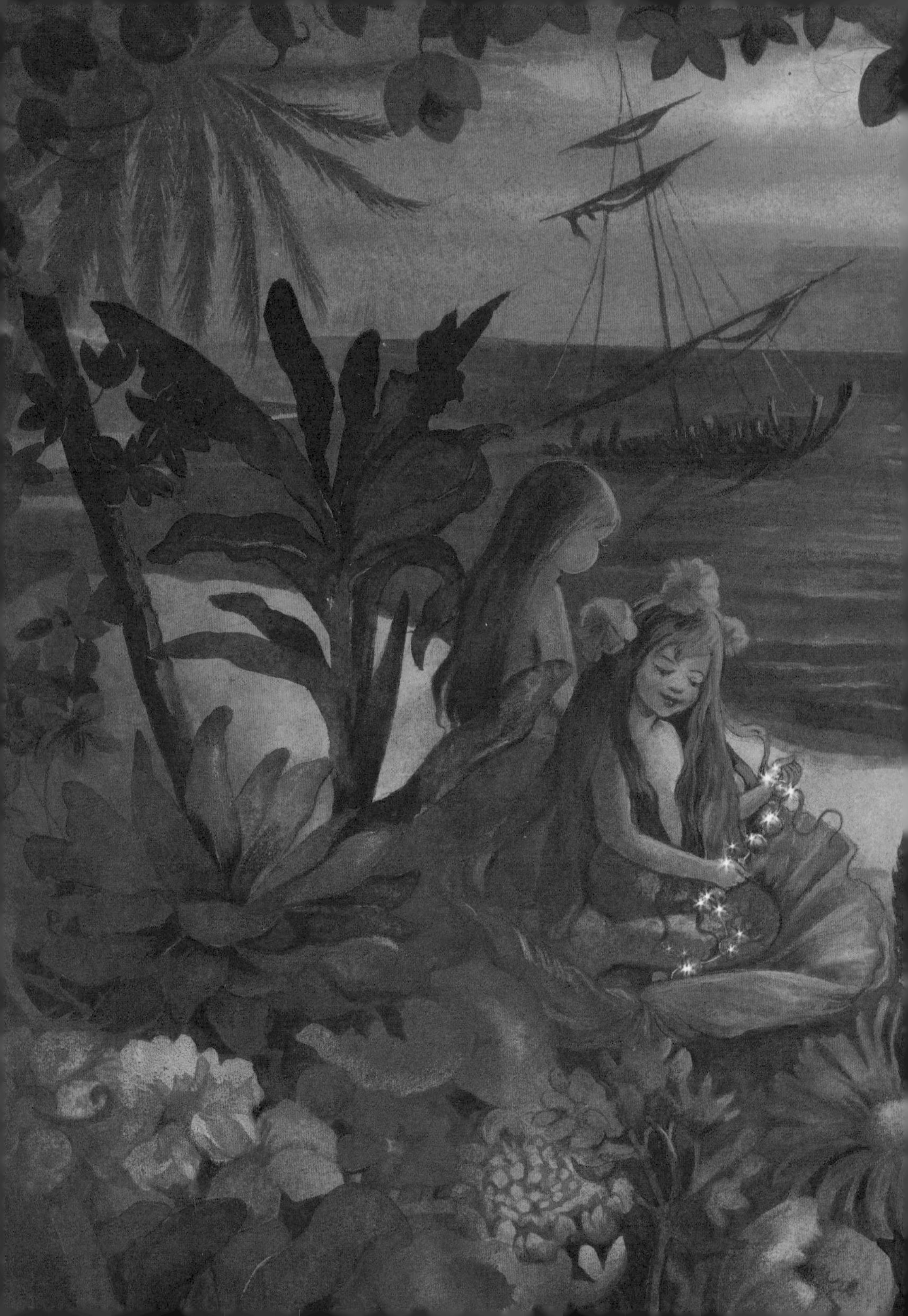

# EASTER

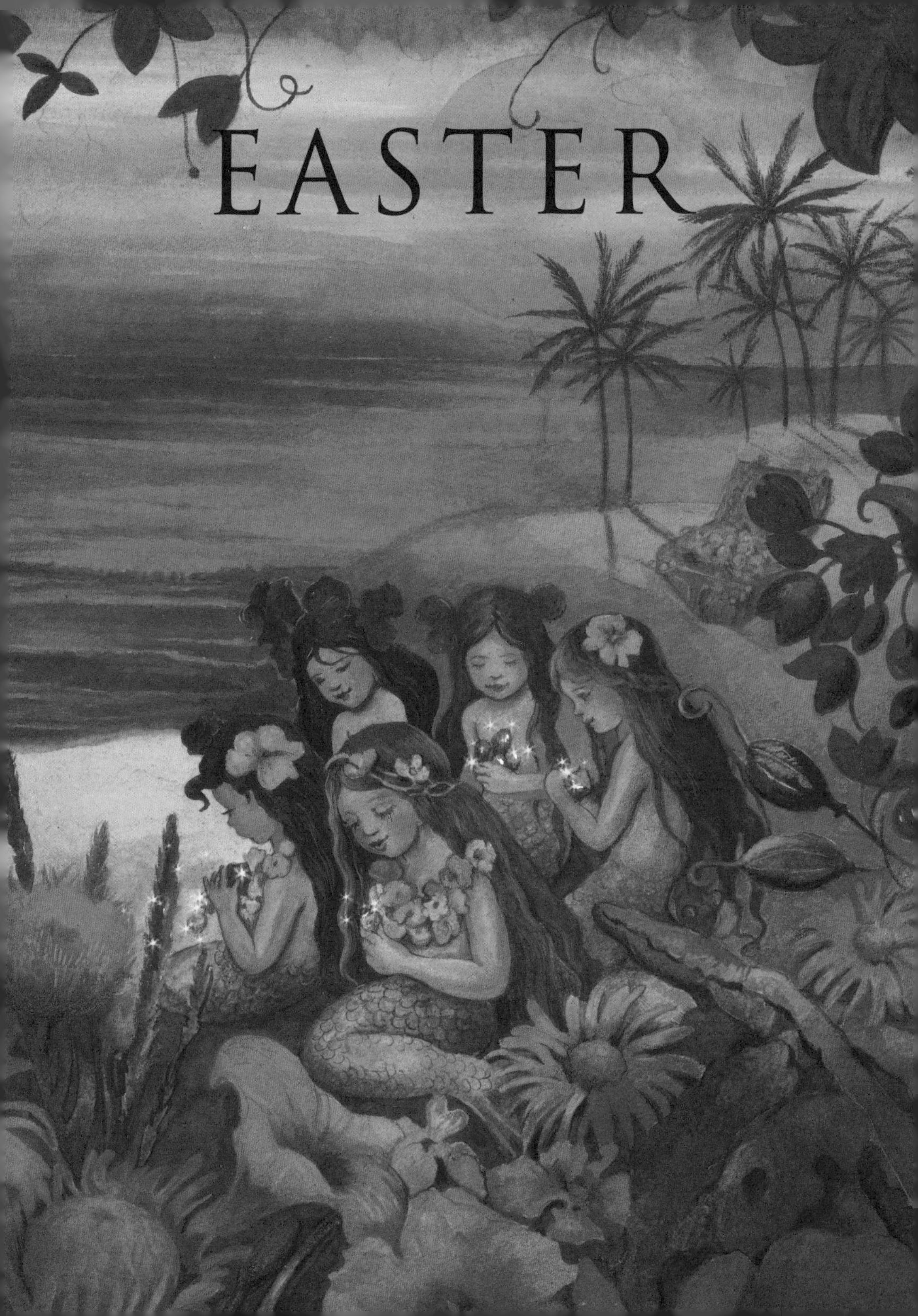

# APRIL

Dear Diary,
It's the Easter Jewel Hunt!
Breana found five beautiful
pearls. Audra found seven lovely
stones.

Tahj isn't interested in
pearls. She just wants
to collect the prettiest
eggs. She says the
chocolate ones are the
best part of Easter!

# APRIL

Did you have an Easter Egg Hunt
this Easter? How many Easter eggs did
you find? Write about your favorite
part of the day:

# APRIL

Dear Diary,

I am so tired, I can hardly write.
We've spent all day cleaning the
underwater gardens. Erin and Tara
were distracted by the beautiful fish
and they kept forgetting why we were
there! Tomorrow, all the older mermaids
come to visit and everything has to be
perfect.

34

Can you draw a picture of some beautiful fish?

# APRIL

Dear Diary, today has been
amazing and all our hard work
was worth it! The gardens were
gorgeous – full of clownfish
and coral trout, seahorses and
starfish.

# APRIL

Try designing your own coral garden –
right here:

# MAY

Alodra
and Callista
and all their friends are
making one another
friendship necklaces.
I'm going to make one
for Celeste.

# MAY

Can you make something special for a
friend today? Show it here:

 # MAY

Dear Diary,

When I am older I want to be just like Oceana. She arrived today in a fabulous seahorse-drawn chariot, wearing a tiara with mother-of-pearl and sea stars. I have never seen anything so beautiful.

# MAY

The seahorses are so quiet and graceful. They're really fish, although they don't look much like fish.
Did you know that seahorse fathers take care of their babies?

# MAY

Dear Diary,

Today, Zana and I have been helping feed the fish. They nibbled our fingers and it was really ticklish. We couldn't stop giggling.

# MAY

What makes you giggle?

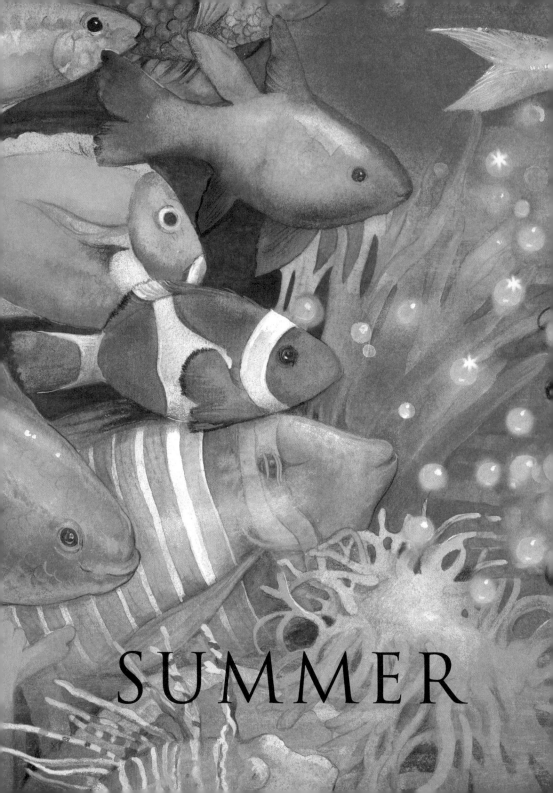

SUMMER

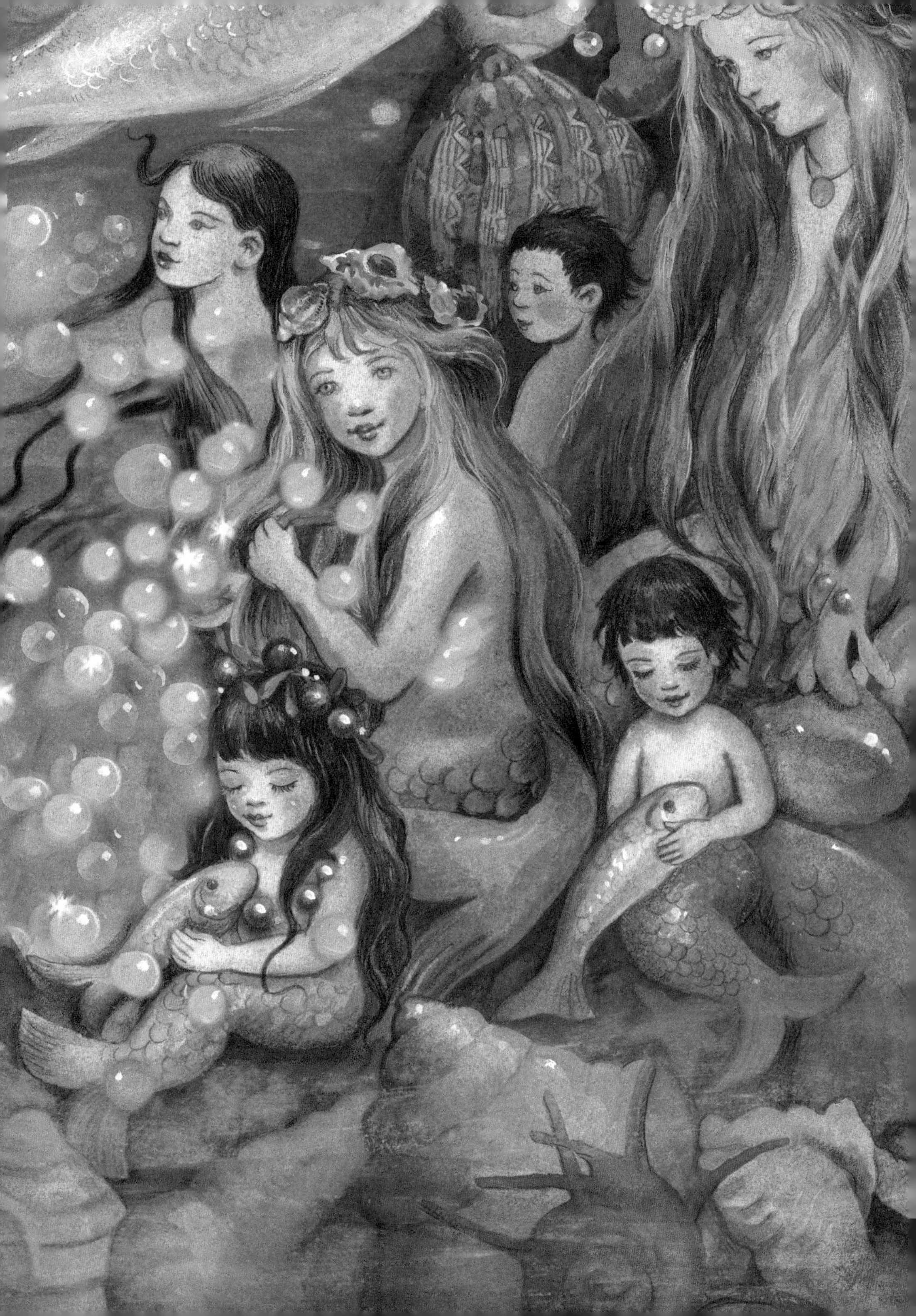

# JUNE

Dear Diary,

I love summer! We have been training for the Mermaid Marathon. It's so much fun. Even though we get tired out, we keep on racing till bedtime.

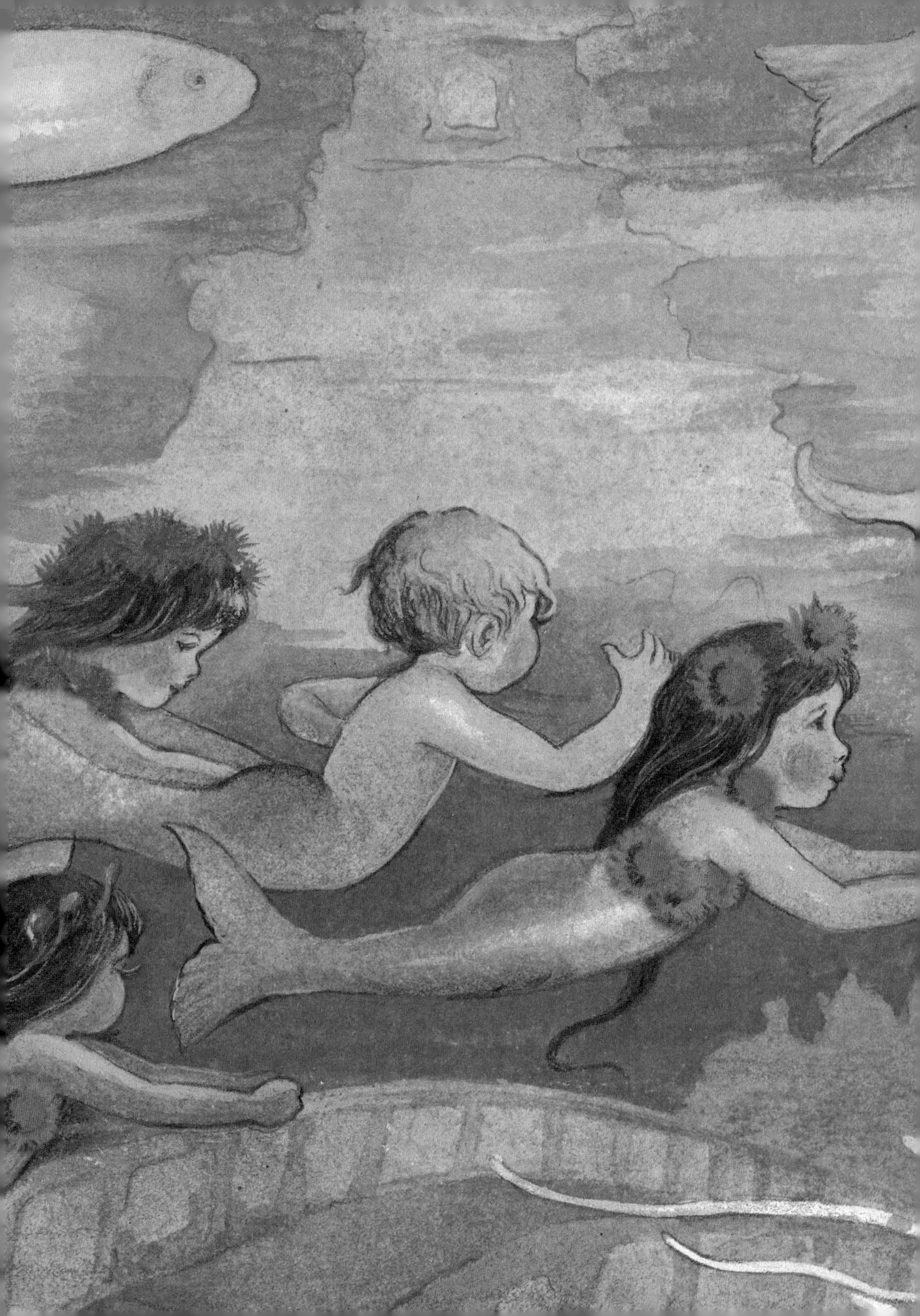

# JUNE

Dear Diary,

I found a mermaid poem at the

underwater library. It's called "The

Mermaids", by Anonymous. Here's

a bit of it:

I have seen the mermaids

swimming in the sea.

Leaping with the dolphins,

racing wild and free.

I have seen the mermaids,

but they didn't see me.

# JUNE

Have you ever seen a dolphin?

Can you draw one?

# JUNE

Dear Diary,

Queen Sula has invited us to the palace for the beginning of July. There is so much to do and I'm so very, very excited. I don't think I'll sleep much tonight.

# JUNE

We have been busy braiding
our hair and practicing our
curtsies — all for Queen Sula
and the July Celebration.

# JULY

Dear Diary,

The big day has finally arrived and Queen Sula is waiting to see us. Rosalind is going to recite a poem, and Breana and I will stick close together so we don't get lost. The palace is enormous.

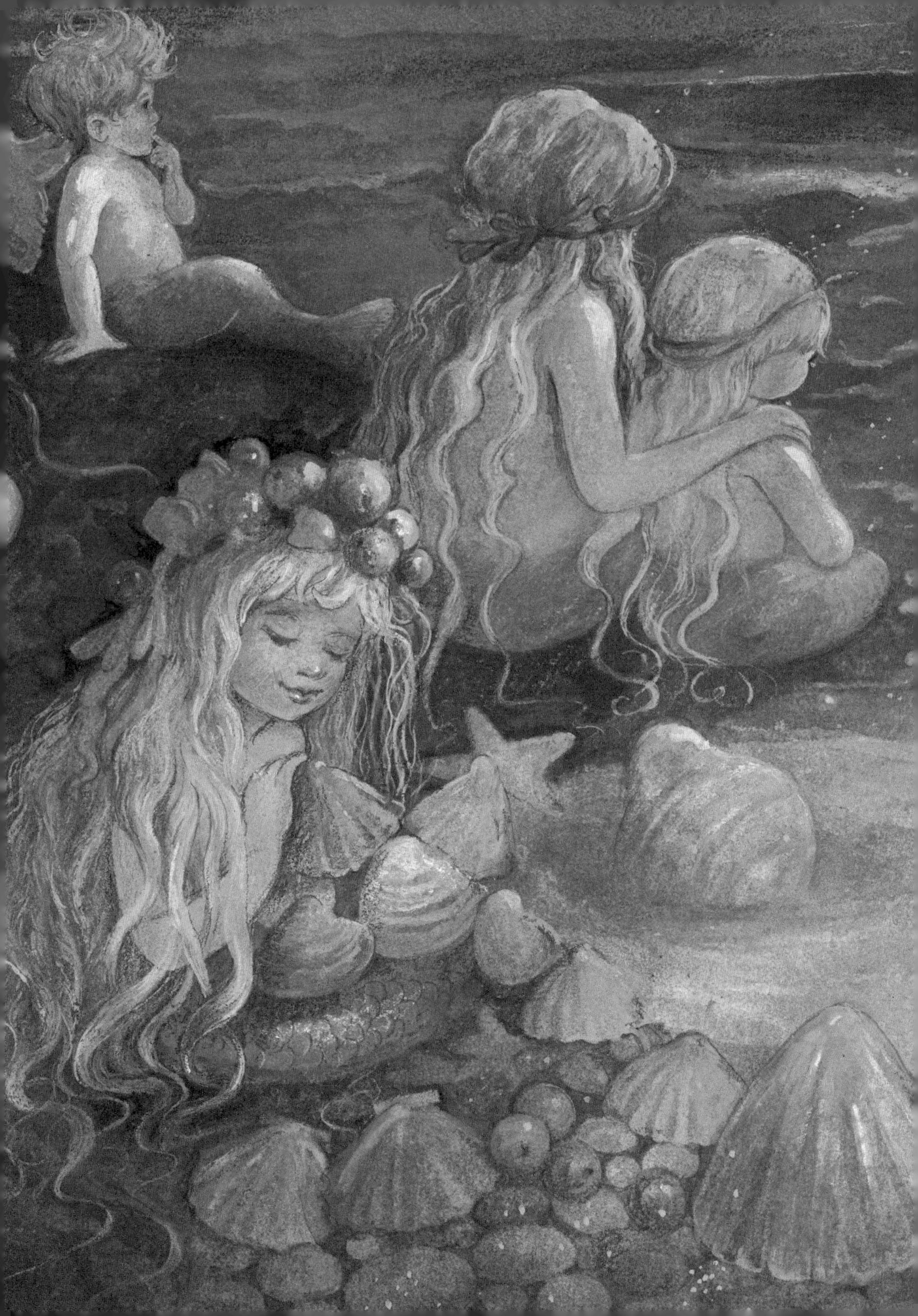

# JULY

Dear Diary,

What an amazing time we had.

We swam through the Coral Forest and over the Emerald Bridge into the Underwater Palace. Glow fish lit our way. They were like magical underwater lanterns – but they moved!

# JULY

There was music and dancing and the most delicious treats – sugared coral, sea gumdrops, seaweed sticks, and sea berry juice. Yummy.

# AUGUST

Dear Diary,

July just flew by, so I'm sorry I haven't been writing. Here is a picture of Queen Sula. Her crown of sea pearls is glowing. Isn't she beautiful? I want to look like her when I grow up.

# AUGUST

Could you draw a picture of
a mermaid queen that looks
just like you?

# AUGUST

Anna and I have been swimming under the stars. We've been trying to decide the best thing about this summer. Summer is my favorite time of year. The days are long and the nights are dark and warm. It's very hard, but I think meeting Queen Sula was the best time!

# AUGUST

What is the most exciting thing you can remember happening so far this summer? Can you write about it?

# AUGUST

Dear Diary,

I found this lovely poem in a book.

It's called "The Sea Maid" and it's from a

play called "A Midsummer Night's Dream"

by William Shakespeare:

"They bring me coral and amber clear.

But when the stars in heaven appear,

their music ceases, they glide away.

They swim for their grottos

across the bay."

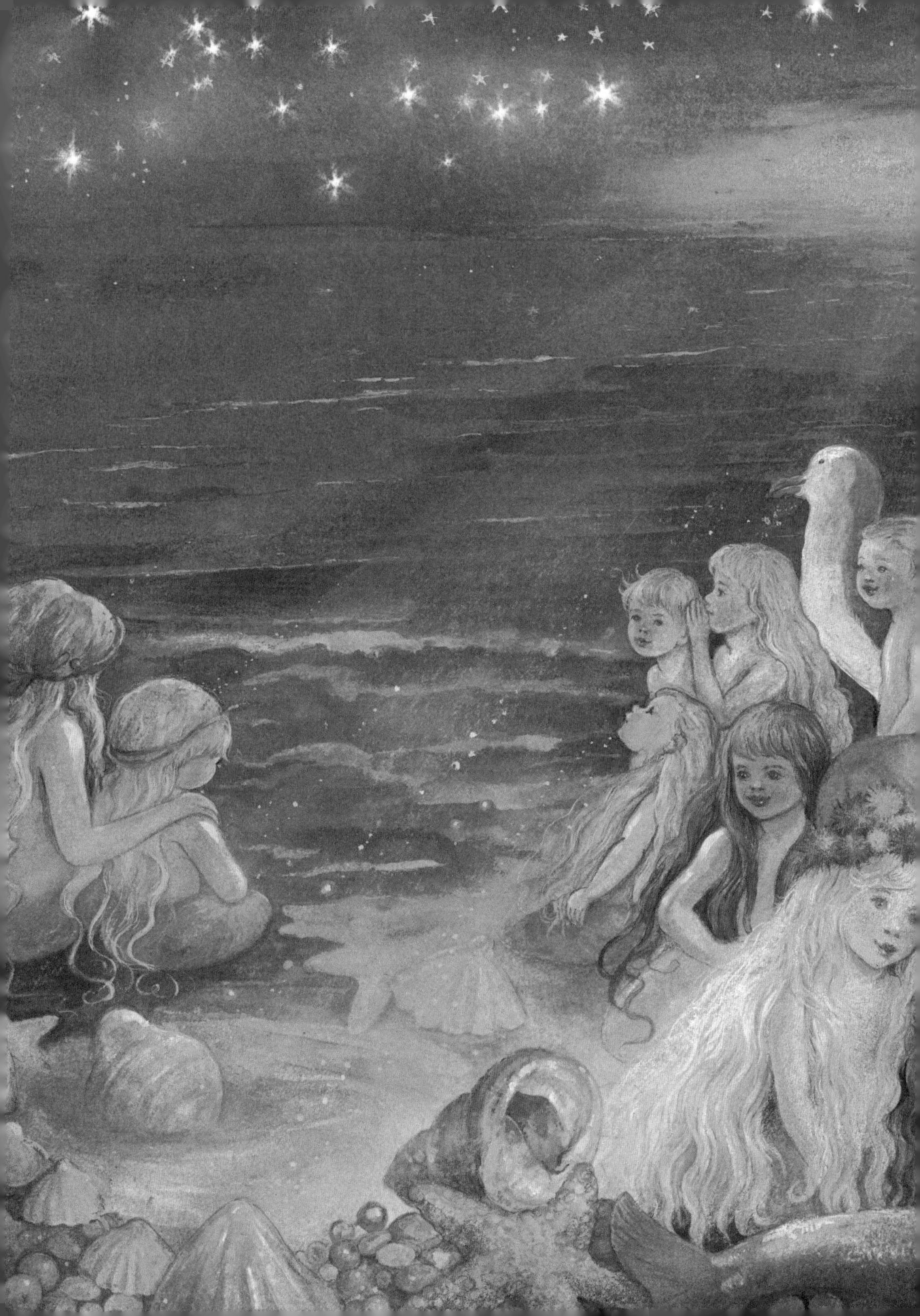

# FALL

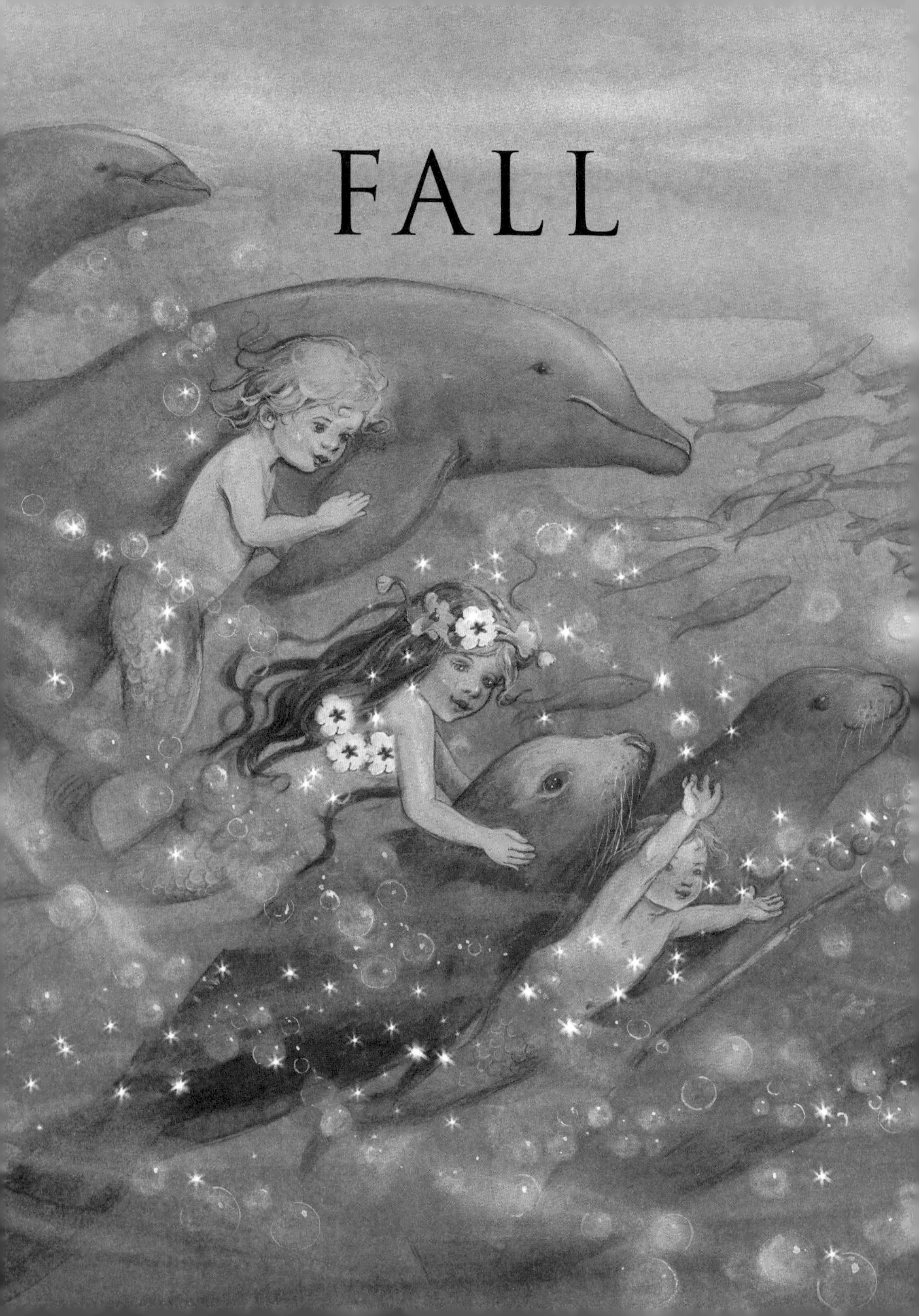

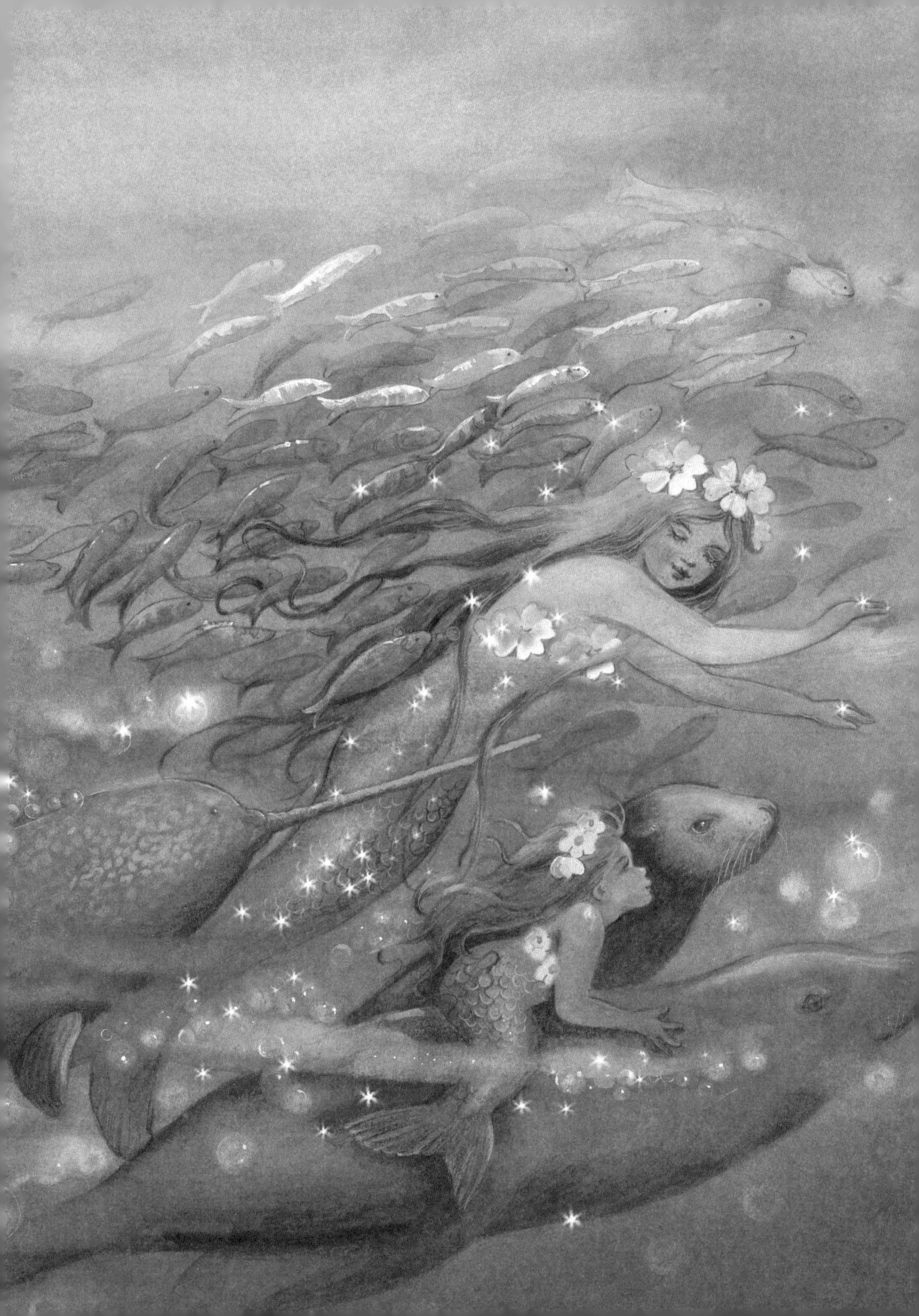

# SEPTEMBER

Dear Diary,

The summer nights have
ended and Fall has come. We
will be starting lessons again
soon - diving, singing, coral
reef cleaning, hair braiding.

# SEPTEMBER

Things to remember for the
first day at school:

# SEPTEMBER

Dear Diary,

Aguina and Netty found some
starfish today. We have been
having starfish races. We were all
cheering them on. Netty discovered
that if she tickled her starfish, it
moved more quickly. Aguina's kept
stopping for a rest! I think it was
too tired to race.

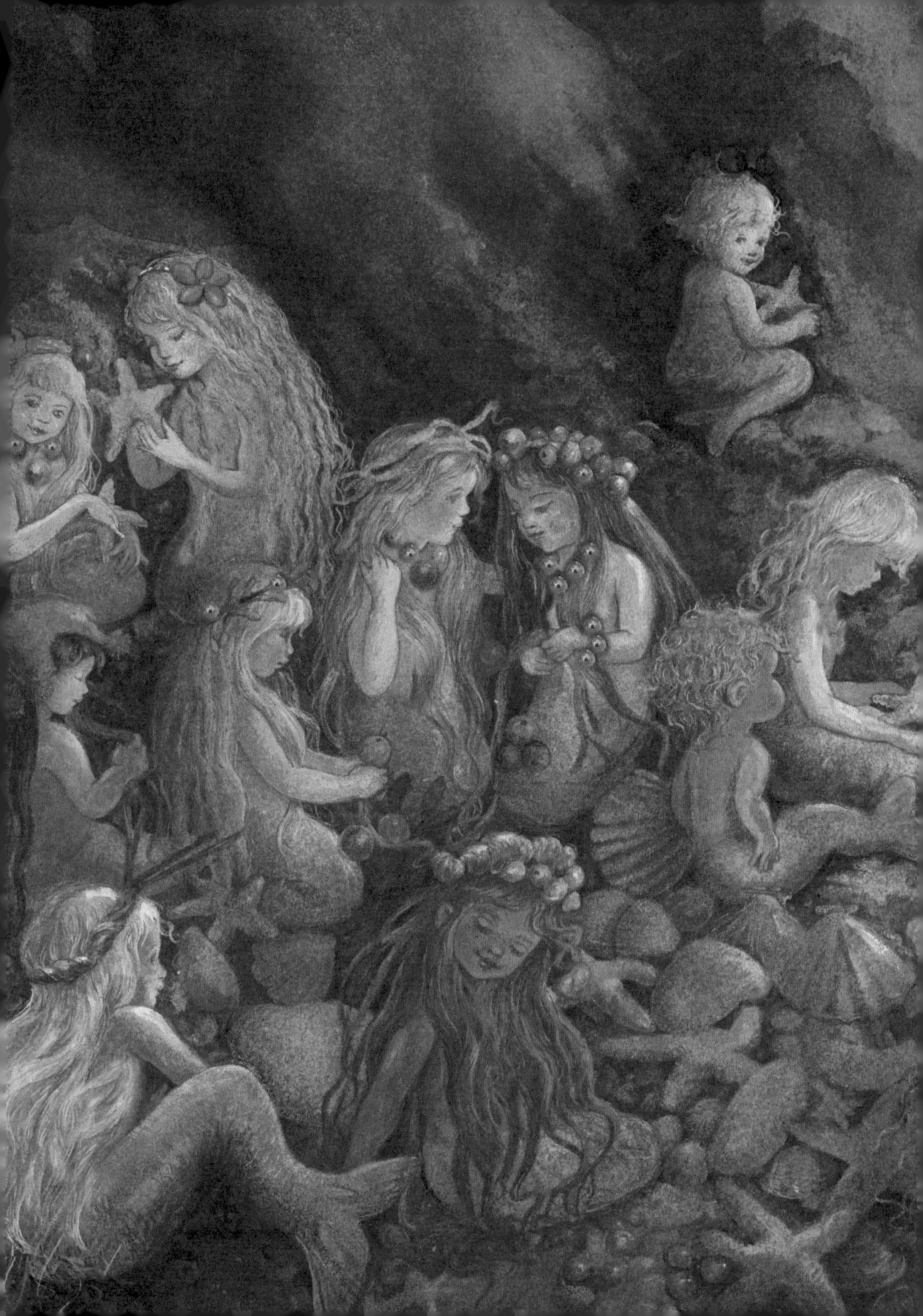

# SEPTEMBER

Dear Diary,

We've been playing hide –
and –seek with the little
ones. Octavia and Atticus
were hidden so well, we
couldn't find them – and
then they fell asleep! They
only woke up when they
were hungry.

# SEPTEMBER

Have you ever eaten food from the sea?
Fish? Clams? Lobster? What are your
favorite seafoods?

# OCTOBER

Dear Diary,

Mermaids are famous for three things: swimming, singing, and our long, long hair! Did you know that we wash it every day and spend hours brushing and braiding it?

70

# OCTOBER

How do you like to wear your hair?
Short, long, curly, straight, braided?
Draw a picture of yourself in your
favorite hairstyle:

# OCTOBER

Dear Diary,

After lessons, we have been
trying to make a list of all the
sea creatures we have seen.
There are starfish, seahorses,
sea urchins, sea anemones, and scallops,
oysters, shrimp, crabs, lobsters, and
all kinds of colorful fishes. There are
seals and sea lions and dolphins.

# OCTOBER

Can you name all the sea creatures you have seen? Try making a list of them here:

# OCTOBER

Have you ever imagined a new sea creature? Is it big? Tiny? Has it got legs? Fins? What color is it? Show us:

# OCTOBER

Now you can design your very own
sea shell to go with your own sea
creature!

# NOVEMBER

Dear Diary,

Owww!!! I got bitten on the bottom by a crab today!! He had sharp claws.

# NOVEMBER

Here's a bit of another lovely
mermaid poem:
"I have seen mermaids
riding seaward on the waves
Combing the white hair
of the waves blown back"
T. S. Eliot

77

# NOVEMBER

Dear Diary,

There was the most amazing storm last night — lightning and thunder! It's a mermaid secret that a thunderstorm often means the birth of a new merbaby.

# NOVEMBER

Can you remember what a big storm sounds like? Was it really noisy? During the day or nighttime? Were you scared? Write about it:

# NOVEMBER

Dear Diary,

I was right! There is a new merbaby!
She's called Starchild, and she's
beautiful. Everyone has heard the news
and wants to join in the celebrations
and say thank you for her safe arrival.

# THANKSGIVING

Are you celebrating Thanksgiving?
What are you thankful for? What will
you have for dinner? Write about your
Thanksgiving:

# WINTER

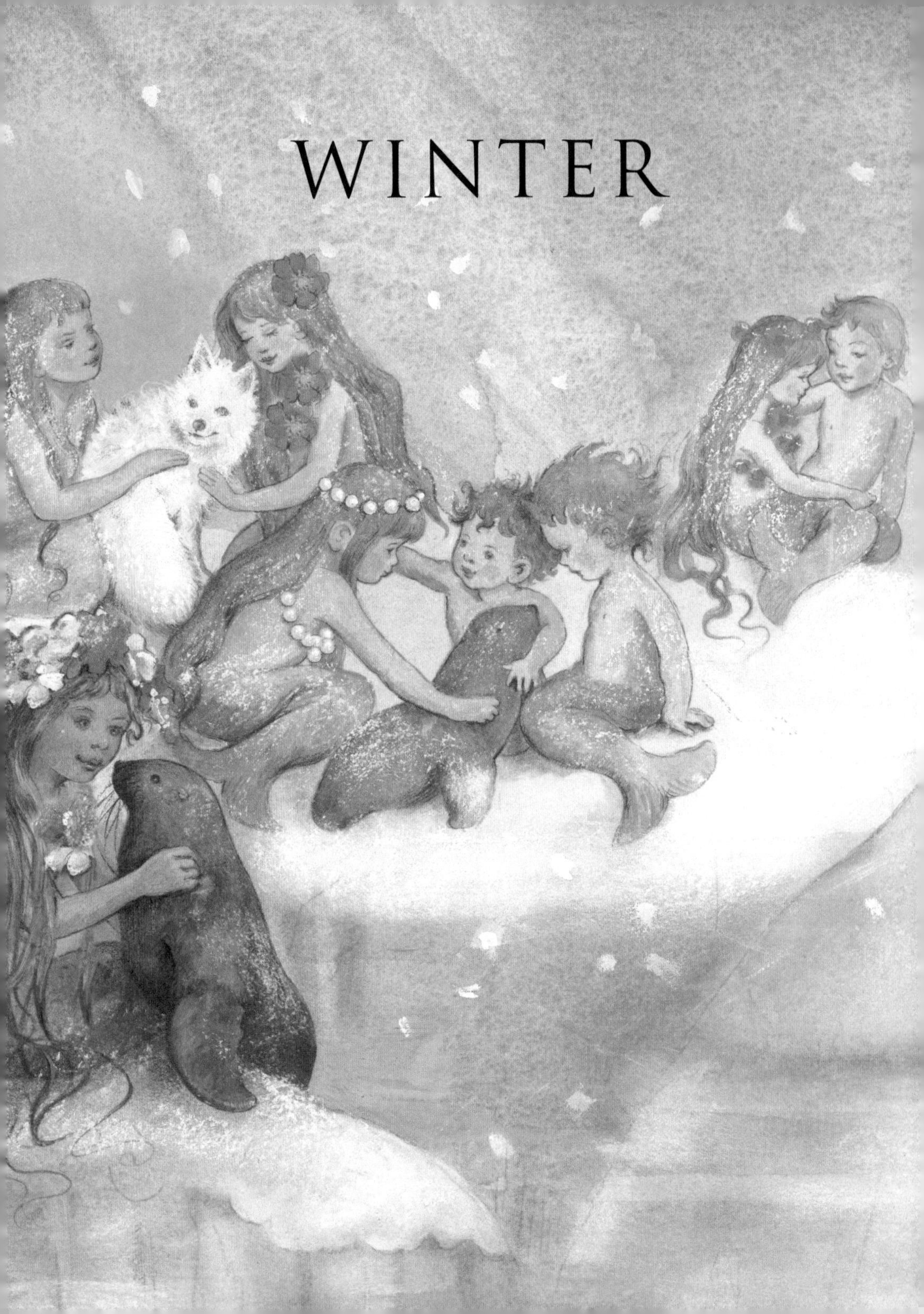

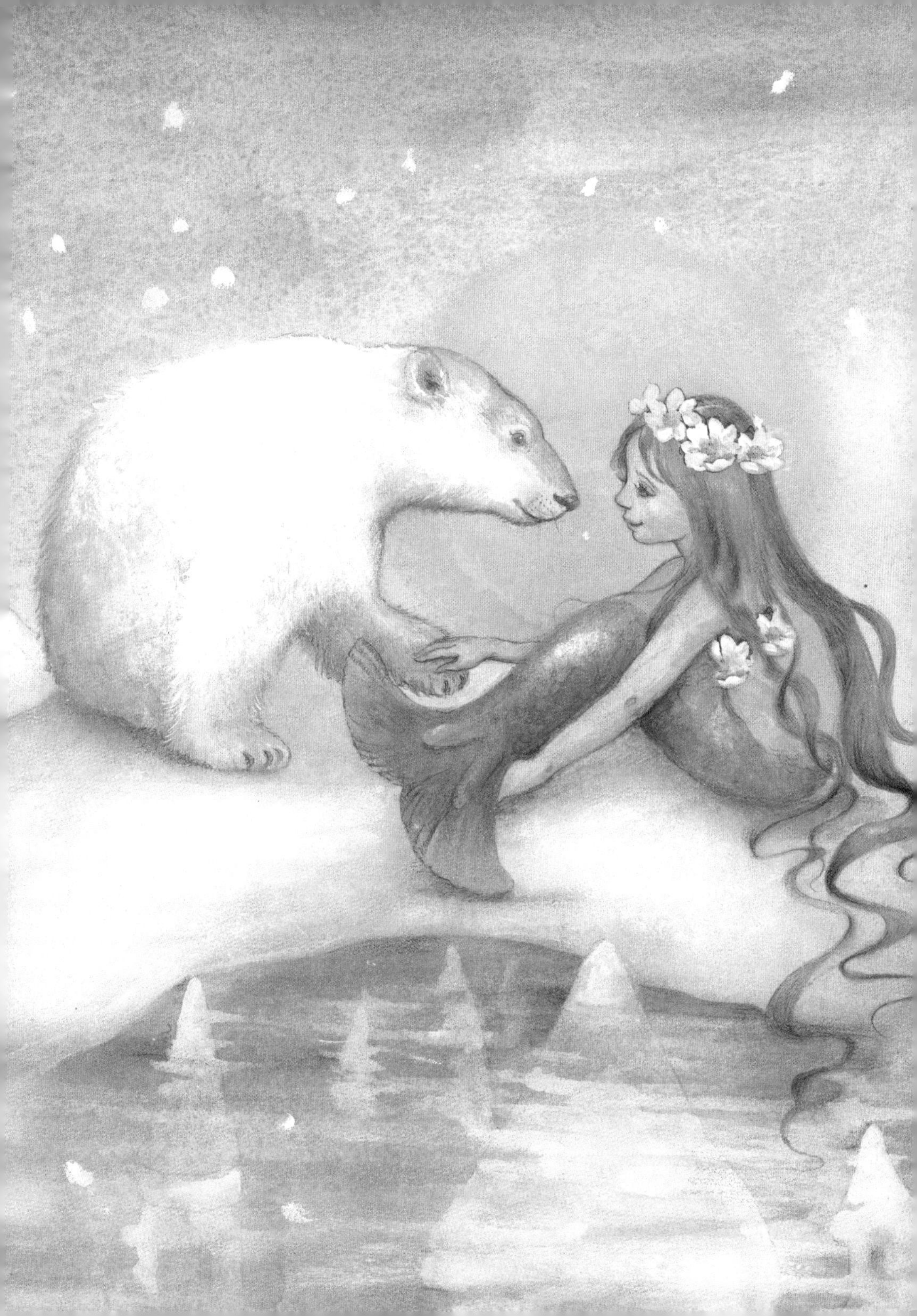

# DECEMBER

Dear Diary,

Big news!! King Neptune is coming
to visit! He wants to celebrate
Starchild's birth with us.

I am so excited I think I might burst!

# DECEMBER

This might be a good time to write your
Christmas letter and send it to Santa.

# DECEMBER

Dear Diary,

Oh, the celebration was
glorious. King Neptune
tells the most amazing sea
stories. We spent hours in
the cave, listening to all his
tales, feasting, and playing
at his feet.

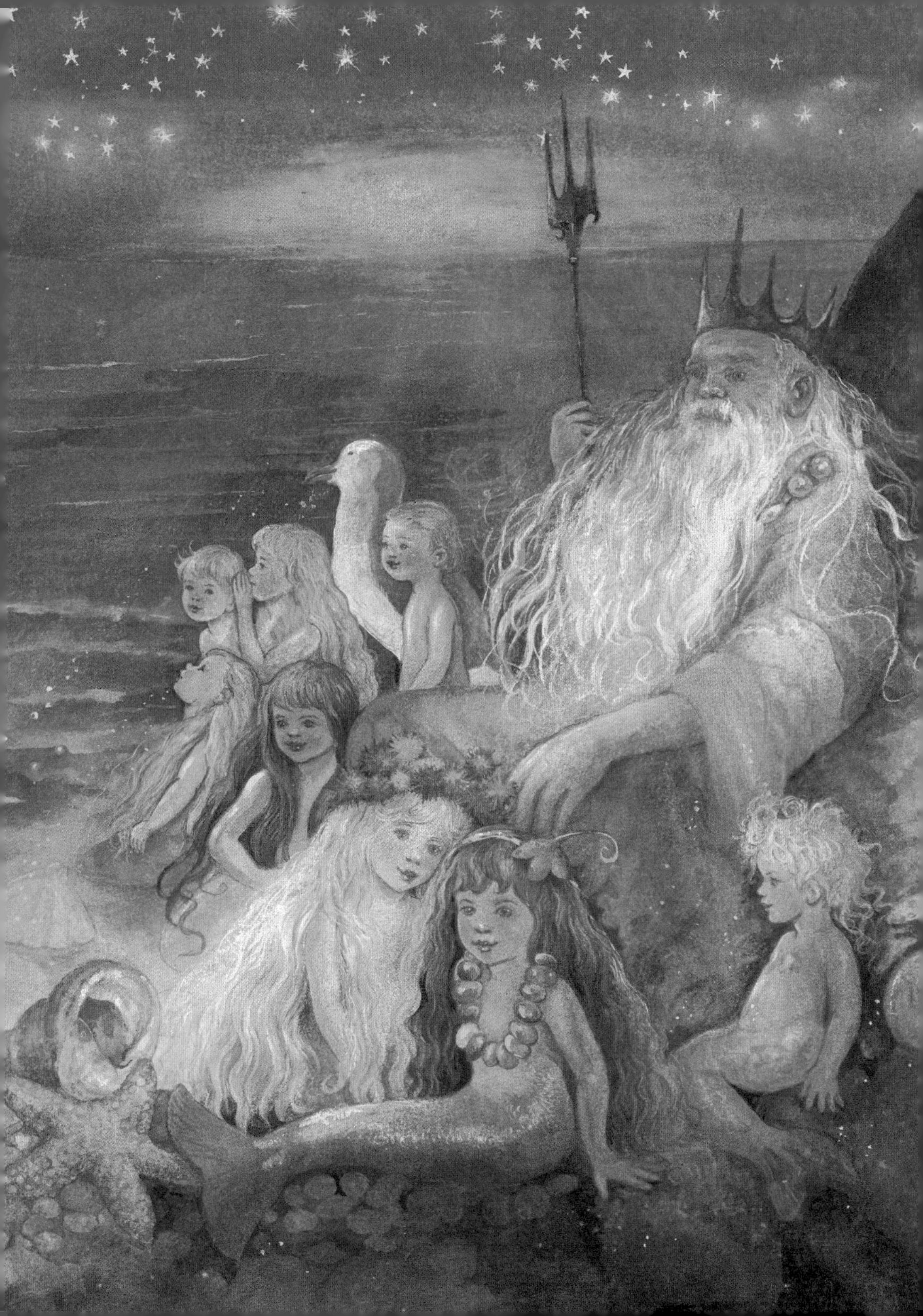

# CHRISTMAS

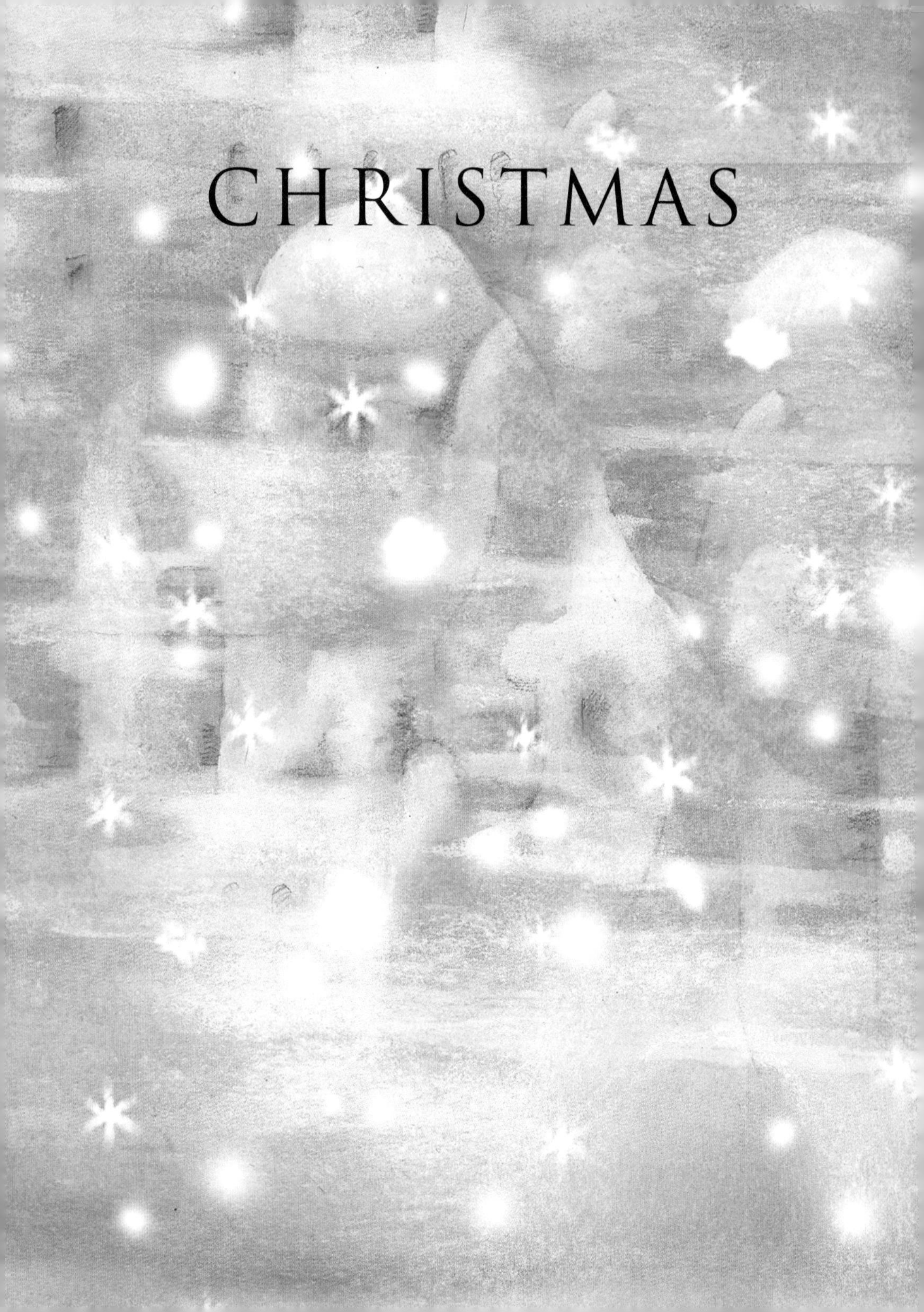

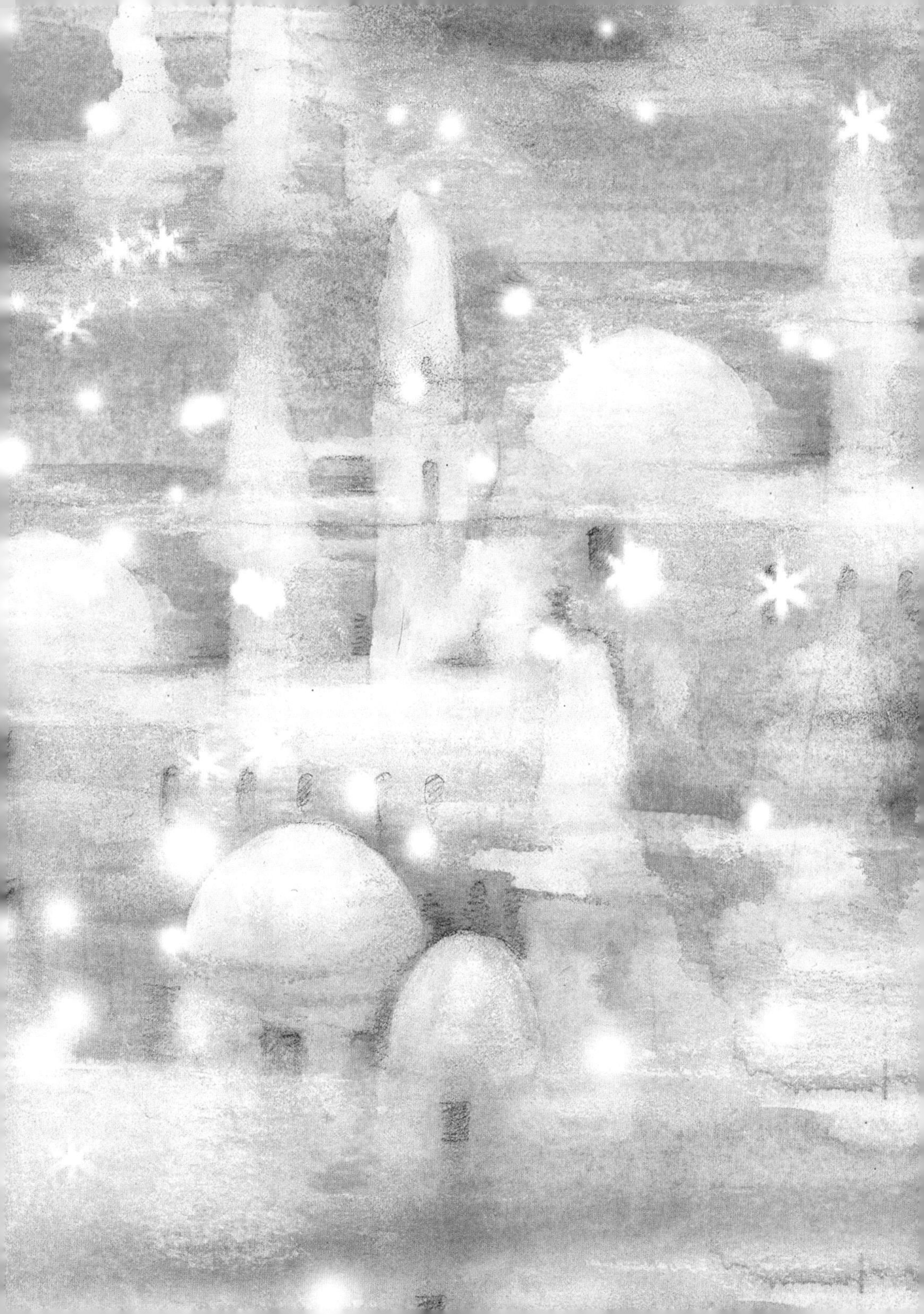

# CHRISTMAS

Dear Diary,

King Neptune told us about a winter festival that some people celebrate called Christmas. He said the people exchange gifts.

Harmony has been stringing shells together to make a rattle for Starchild.

# CHRISTMAS

Have you made any Christmas presents?
What did you give to your family to
show them how much you love them?

# NEXT YEAR

Mermaid Resolutions for next year:

I will help keep the coral reefs clean.

I will look after the merbabies.

I will keep practicing my diving.

What are your New year's Resolutions?

# NEXT YEAR

## MY NEW YEAR'S RESOLUTIONS ARE:

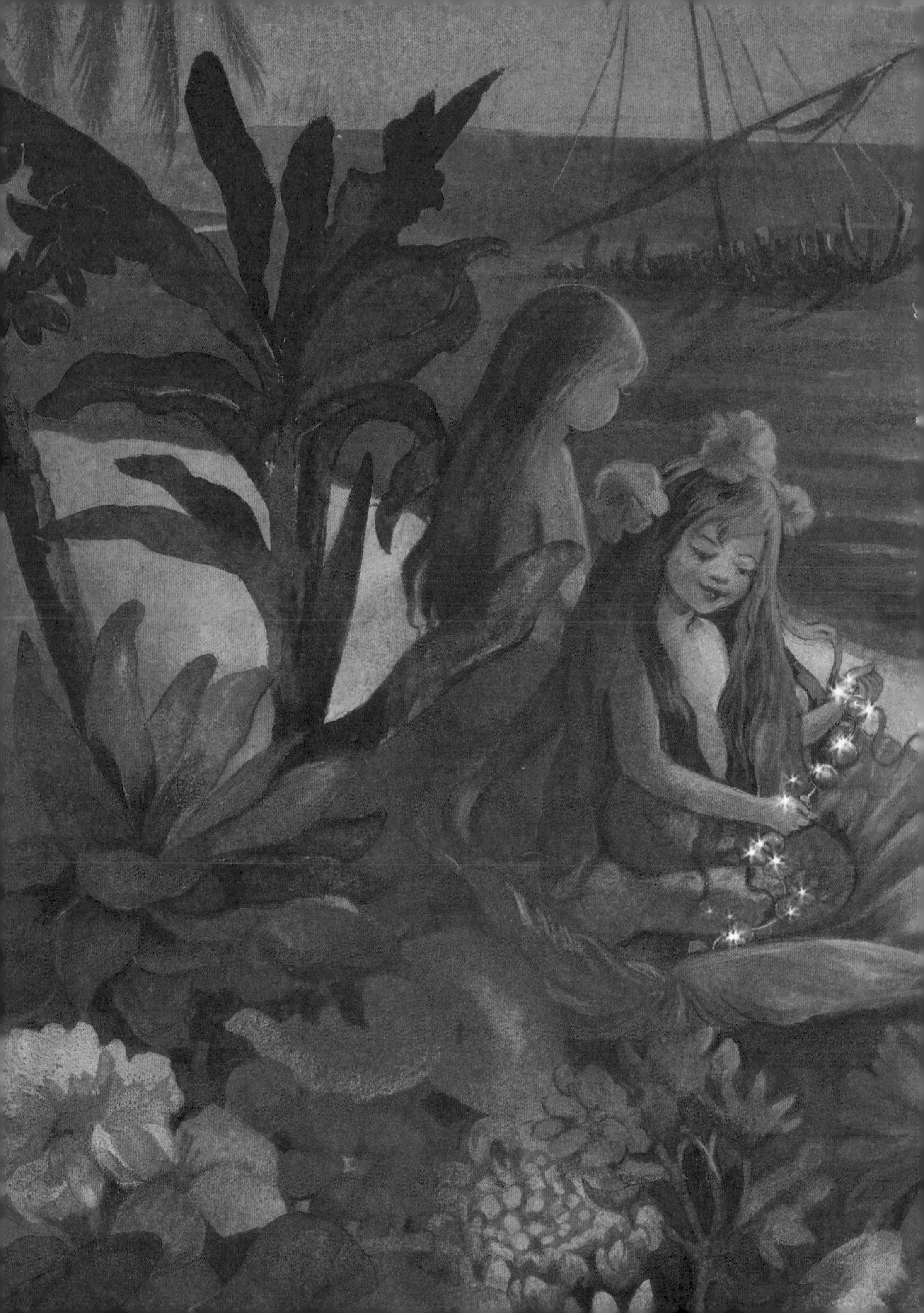